The TARTAN TRAMPOLINE and the SUPERHEROES

Written by
JENNIFER BAKER

Illustrated by
SARAH CAMPBELL

The Tartan Trampoline and the Superheroes

ISBN 978-1-9993668-8-9 (paperback)

Second printing October 2021

Published by
Mòr Media Limited
Argyll, Scotland

www.mormedia.co.uk
Book design by Helen Crossan

Other books in *The Tartan Trampoline* series

The Tartan Trampoline and the Pirate
The Tartan Trampoline and the Red Shoes

For Mànas

It was the Easter holidays, and Tilly had arrived all the way from Manchester to meet up with her cousins, Manny and Effie, in Glasgow. They were going to visit their grandmother's island like they always did in the holidays.

The next day, they caught the train that left the city and travelled through mountain passes and by the side of lochs till they came to the ferry.

There, Allan the ferryman was waiting to take them across the water to their favourite place—the island.

They loved the island because they could swim and fish and climb rocks, but mostly because that's where the Tartan Trampoline was. Nobody else knew how *magic* that trampoline was. It was a secret belonging to Manny, Effie and Tilly.

Allan always joked, 'No, not you three *again*! You gonnae run wild for a few weeks? Drive your granny mad?'

The children laughed. They knew he didn't mean it.

By the way, their grandmother was called Shayjay. Why she was called that is a mystery. Perhaps Shayjay knew, but she never told.

Shayjay was waiting for them as usual and, as she drove them to her house, she said, 'Is it straight onto the trampoline again?'

'Yes!' they all yelled with delight.

'Right! I'll get the tea on, then after that it's bed. It's a long journey from Glasgow, and you don't want to be tired tomorrow.'

The children bounced and turned cartwheels and belly-flopped till Shayjay called them in and soon they were tucked up cosily in bed.

'I hope it's really windy in the morning,' whispered Manny, but the other two were sound asleep.

5

When they awoke the next morning,

there was a huge wind howling round the

house. They were delighted. It was so early it

was still dark. They could see the moon through the

windows in the bedroom roof.

'Let's go,' said Manny, 'but remember,

really quietly.'

They were very good at tiptoeing down the stairs, and soon they were running around the field at the front of the house being blown about by the wind.

'Okay, come on!' said Manny. They climbed the steps up to the trampoline but this time there was no bouncing.

They lay flat on their tummies and peered over the edge. This bit was always a wee bit scary. Then the wind picked the Tartan Trampoline up, and swirled them into the starry sky. By the light of the moon, the children could see the silvery loch far, far below. Then the sun rose over the water, and the whole world turned pink and golden.

'It looks as though we're going to land there,' said Manny, pointing to an island that had a very high mountain on it.

'There are people on the beach,' said Effie, screwing up her eyes so that she could see better.'

'Oh yes,' said Tilly, 'they're all *fighting!*'

The trampoline once again floated gently down and, when the children climbed off it, they saw the strangest bunch of people they had ever seen before in their whole lives.

'For goodness' sake!' breathed Manny.

'What the heck!' whispered Effie.

'Who ARE they?' yelled Tilly.

'Shhh,'

said the other

two but they had

already been spotted.

Even though the fighters

were fully engrossed in their

fighting, as fighters usually are,

they had seen the trampoline coming

down, and had stopped their fighting to

watch it land.

There were two grown-ups and four teenagers.

9

One grown-up was clothed from top to toe in a very, very tight tartan Lycra suit and the other also had on a tight Lycra suit but his was black and shiny. He had Harris Tweed underpants on top and a Harris Tweed cape.

Manny said politely, 'Hello, I'm Manny and this is my sister Effie and my cousin Tilly. We've just dropped by for a wee while.'

'Hello,' said the tartan one, rubbing his sore hands, 'ah'm Super Shug. Pleased tae meet yez.'

'And I am Fantastic Farquhar,'
said the tweed one, 'and these
are my trainee superheroes.'

The teenagers, who were also in shiny black Lycra but without the tweed pants, looked at the children without smiling or saying hello but that is quite normal for teenagers—even superteenagers.

'Are you really … s-s-superheroes?' Manny could barely even say the word he was so excited.

'Well, yes, of course,' said Fantastic Farquhar. 'I am Edinburgh's superhero and Super Shug is Glasgow's _ex_-superhero.' Farquhar laughed in a not-very-nice way. Super Shug looked at him angrily.

'An' whose fault is that?' he shouted. 'Ye've taken ma superpowers *away*, which is against a' the rules and ethics of superheroes jist because you wanted tae show aff tae these trainees here. What kind of an example dae ye think ye are showin' to them?' The trainee superheroes looked bored and a bit grumpy.

13

'Oh, I can't be bothered with any more of this,' said Farquhar. 'Come, boys and girls. We're going home. Manny, Effie, Tilly, it's been very nice meeting you.'

And lifting himself up onto his very elegant toes, he flew gracefully up into the morning sky, the tweed cape flowing out behind. The trainees, after a few false starts and bumpings down on their bottoms, finally got up into the air and flew off after him.

Super Shug was devastated. 'Whit's Glesca gonnae dae noo with nae superhero?'

'Does every town have a superhero?' asked Manny.

'Naw, sonny, but every city does, and Glesca's a city, an' noo it disnae huv wan, an' that's a disaster. Us superheroes catch criminals, and pick crashed cars oot o' the river, and rescue people frae a' kinds o' dangers.'

He sat down heavily on a big rock and put his head in his hands.

The children sat down beside him. 'Can you tell us what happened?' asked Tilly gently.

'Aye weel, ah micht as weel. Ye see, ah flew tae this island tae dae a bit o' mountain climbin' …'

'Why don't you just actually fly up the mountain?' interrupted Effie.

'Trainin', hen. Ye've got tae keep yersel fit in this job. Ye niver ken when ye're gaun tae need tae dae a bit o' climbin', or hangin' frae trees, or liftin' heavy folks oot frae windaes when their hooses are on fire.'

Effie nodded.

'So ah'm climbin' this mountain here,' he nodded up at the huge mountain in the middle of the island.

'Wow, that's high!' said Tilly.

'Aye hen, ah dinna mind admitting it's no an easy climb.

'Onyway, ah'm aboot hauf way up when in flies thon Farquhar wi' his posh Edinburgh ways and his trainees—whit a crowd of miseries they are—an' he tries tae push me aff the mountain. Jist showin' aff, ye ken. Tryin' tae look big in front of his trainees.

'Ah hud my powers switched aff so's ah widnae be tempted tae cheat on the hard bits, and ah didnae huv time tae turn them oan again. Took me by surprise, like, an' ah fell aff the mountain!'

'No!' gasped the children.

'Did you hurt yourself?' asked Manny.

'Naw, son. It wis okay. Ah hud time tae turn ma powers oan afore ah hit the rocks but ah tell ye—ah wis that mad! Ah jist swooped straight up thon mountain again and gave Farquhar a big punch on the nose. Well, ye ken, wan thing led tae anither an', afore ye know it, we wis baith fighting, like the stupid eejits we are—but then Farquhar went too far.'

'What did he do?' said Effie.

'He took away ma superpowers!'

'Can he do that?' asked Manny.

'Aye—a' superheroes can. We need to be able to in case we come across wan o' they evil superpeople but ye're only allowed tae use it in very special cases—not jist tae show aff tae yer trainees like thon Farquhar did.'

'Will he come back to help you?' asked Manny.

'Nae chance, son. He's too proud and onyway, he cannae. It's against the super rules. Once ye've taken the power away, ye cannae give it back to the same person. Naw, ah'm finished as a superhero noo. Oh, poor Glesca.' A big tear ran down Super Shug's cheek.

'Can you never get them back?' asked Tilly.

'Aye—if another superhero passes by. But that's no likely tae happen, is it?'

They all sat together on the beach feeling absolutely miserable.

Suddenly Manny had a thought. It was such a good thought that his heart began to beat very fast. He stood up in front of Super Shug and shouted, 'What about a super *thing*?'

'Eh? Sorry son, ah'm nae with ye there.'

'Can you get powers from a super *thing*?'

Effie and Tilly realised what he meant. 'Manny, be careful,' said Effie.

'We might be stranded on this island,' said Tilly.

'No, listen! Can you get your superpowers back from our super trampoline?'

Super Shug looked at the Tartan Trampoline. 'Ah see whit ye mean. Yer trampoline there certainly has superpowers. Aye, it's possible, but it widnae be super onymair because a' its superness wid be in *me*.'

'Never mind!' yelled Manny. 'Try it. You need to do it for all the people in Glasgow.'

'Well, if ye're sure.'

Tilly and Effie didn't look sure at all. 'I hope he knows what he's doing,' whispered Tilly to Effie.

'So do I,' said Effie. 'I don't want to live on this island forever. Actually, I'm ready to go home.' She looked a bit miserable as she said this.

'Me too,' said Tilly, 'but I suppose it has to be done for the people of Glasgow.' She looked miserable too. Manny, on the other hand, was jumping with excitement.

'Go! Go!' he yelled again.

Super Shug climbed onto the trampoline and lay down on his tummy. The tartan of the trampoline gradually changed to merge with the tartan of his suit so that he disappeared completely. The trampoline rose jerkily high into the air, gave a huge squeaky sigh, and returned softly to the ground.

Nothing happened for a minute or two and the children became very nervous. Then, suddenly, from the middle of the trampoline, rose Super Shug. Up into the air he went, his tartan suit glowing.

'Way-hay!' he cheered, and the children cheered too.

It was lovely to see him so happy. He flew around for a while, turning somersaults in the air and whirling around the trees, until he flew towards them and landed lightly on the beach. 'Weel, ah huv tae thank you children very much.' He looked at the trampoline, which now looked very ordinary.

'Ah'm awfy sorry aboot yer trampoline but.'

'We wanted to go home,' said Effie sadly.

'We still can!' shouted Manny. 'Super Shug can take us now!'

'Of course!' said Super Shug. 'Ah wisnae thinkin'. Climb oan!'

The three climbed up the steps to the trampoline and, with no effort at all, Super Shug lifted the trampoline and flew up into the clear blue sky with it. Once again, the children could see the beautiful loch far below. In the distance, they could just make out Shayjay's house.

And then they realised that there was someone flying alongside. It was Fantastic Farquhar. He took hold of the other side of the trampoline.

'Ye came back!' shouted Super Shug through the wind.

'Yes,' said Farquhar. 'I nearly didn't, but I wanted to say that I'm awfully sorry for what I did.'

'Och, nae bother,' said Super Shug. 'Thanks to these three here ah got ma powers back again, so nae harm done.'

And together the two superheroes flew them back home again and laid the Tartan Trampoline back in the field in front of Shayjay's house.

'Will you come in for a cup of tea?' said Manny.

'Sorry kids, we've got a lot of work waitin' fur us in Glesca and Edinburgh,' said Super Shug.

'One minute, Shug,' said Fantastic Farquhar. He leapt onto the trampoline and, placing his hands right on the spot in the middle, closed his eyes.

The children watched in amazement as, little by little, coming out from the centre spot in rays, the trampoline became tartan again.

'How did you do that?' gasped Manny with delight.

Farquhar winked, 'Just a wee superhero trick. I'm sorry that you children had to see two superheroes behaving so badly.'

'Come oan!' shouted Super Shug, who was hovering above Shayjay's house. 'We've a lot o' work tae dae!'

'Coming,' said Fantastic Farquhar and, with a final wave to the children, he joined Super Shug above the chimneys, and the two superheroes flew higher and higher, until they were completely out of sight.

'This is actually brilliant!' said Effie.

'I know,' said Tilly, stroking the glowing tartan.

'Fantastic Farquhar is fantastic,' said Manny

'I hope Shayjay isn't awake,' said Effie. We've been away for half the night and a whole day. And the magic was out of the trampoline for a while.'

'Oh yes,' said Tilly. 'She might have called the police or the mountain rescue.'

'She'll be fine,' said Manny, although he was feeling a bit nervous too. 'Fantastic Farquhar put the magic back.'

Still the children crossed the field slowly and nervously. The door opened, and there was Shayjay standing in her pyjamas. 'Come in my lovely children. It's too early to be out. Breakfast is ready.'

Manny, Effie and Tilly grinned in delight.

The magic was still there.

Acknowledgements

Many thanks to Arthur Cross, Bob Hay and Lorna MacKinnon who sowed the seeds of a great idea which Sarah Campbell and I immediately took up to produce this series of books.

The children of the island primary school 'road-tested' the stories and made valuable suggestions. Thanks, guys!

Thanks also to Adam Mahon, Ruben Campbell-Paine, Amy Bowman and Issy Budd who acted as models for some of the characters.

Lightning Source UK Ltd.
Milton Keynes UK
UKHW021143021221
394922UK00005B/84